DINNER for SIXTEEN

16 SIXTEEN

Written by Loralee Leavitt
Illustrated by Jim Madsen

16 fishermen at the bay . . .

fish for salmon, shiny and gray.

16 children dig on the shore, . . .

looking for scallops, crabs, and more.

16 women with baskets to carry . . .

go into the forest to pick huckleberries.

16 salmon roast on poles.

Clams, crabs, and scallops bake in the coals.

All the families sit down to eat.

They laugh and talk in the fire's red heat.

When they've eaten every bite,
everybody says goodnight.